"Sis?" said Brother. "On the swimming team?"

"Why not?" said Papa. "Last summer, if I remember correctly, she turned herself into a pretty good little swimmer."

"*Pretty* good?" said Sister. "*Little?*"

"It's just an expression, dear," said Mama. "Papa knows you're a big girl and an excellent swimmer."

"Oh, come off it," said Brother. "No offense, Sis, but you're younger and smaller than all the other cubs who'll be trying out for the team. Let's see now—I'll make the team for my crawl, Cousin Fred will make it for his backstroke, Queenie for her butterfly, and Bonnie for her breaststroke. Unless, that is, Too-Tall and the gang beat us all out."

"You mean," said Sister, "unless *I* beat you all out."

BIG CHAPTER BOOKS

The Berenstain Bears and the Drug Free Zone
The Berenstain Bears and the New Girl in Town
The Berenstain Bears Gotta Dance!
The Berenstain Bears and the Nerdy Nephew
The Berenstain Bears Accept No Substitutes
The Berenstain Bears and the Female Fullback
The Berenstain Bears and the Red-Handed Thief
The Berenstain Bears and the Wheelchair Commando
The Berenstain Bears and the School Scandal Sheet
The Berenstain Bears and the Galloping Ghost
The Berenstain Bears at Camp Crush
The Berenstain Bears and the Giddy Grandma
The Berenstain Bears and the Dress Code
The Berenstain Bears' Media Madness
The Berenstain Bears in the Freaky Funhouse
The Berenstain Bears and the Showdown at Chainsaw Gap
The Berenstain Bears in Maniac Mansion
The Berenstain Bears at the Teen Rock Cafe
The Berenstain Bears and the Bermuda Triangle
The Berenstain Bears and the Ghost of the Auto Graveyard
The Berenstain Bears and the Haunted Hayride
The Berenstain Bears and Queenie's Crazy Crush
The Berenstain Bears and the Big Date
The Berenstain Bears and the Love Match
The Berenstain Bears and the Perfect Crime (Almost)
The Berenstain Bears Go Platinum
The Berenstain Bears and the G-Rex Bones
The Berenstain Bears Lost in Cyberspace
The Berenstain Bears in the Wax Museum
The Berenstain Bears Go Hollywood
The Berenstain Bears and No Guns Allowed
The Berenstain Bears and the Great Ant Attack
The Berenstain Bears Phenom in the Family

The Berenstain Bears

PHENOM IN THE FAMILY

by the Berenstains

A BIG CHAPTER BOOK™

Random House New York

Copyright © 2000 by Berenstain Enterprises, Inc.

www.randomhouse.com/kids
www.berenstainbears.com

Library of Congress Cataloging-in-Publication Data
Berenstain, Stan, 1923–
The Berenstain Bears phenom in the family / by Stan & Jan Berenstain.
   p. cm. — (A big chapter book)
SUMMARY: When Sister Bear tries out for the school swim team and reveals
that she is an extremely talented swimmer, Papa starts to push her too hard.
ISBN 0-679-88952-3 (trade). — ISBN 0-679-98952-8 (lib. bdg.)
[1. Swimming—Fiction.] I. Berenstain, Jan, 1923–   . II. Title.
PZ7.B4483 Bfed 2000 [Fic]—dc21 99-052550

Printed in the United States of America October 2000 10 9 8 7 6 5 4 3 2 1

BIG CHAPTER BOOKS and colophon are trademarks of
Berenstain Enterprises, Inc.
RANDOM HOUSE and colophon are registered trademarks of
Random House, Inc.

Contents

Chapter 1
The Rumor

"A rumor's going around that there's gonna be a special announcement before classes start today," said Barry Bruin.

"It ain't no rumor, it's a fact," said Too-Tall Grizzly. "And I know what the announcement's about."

The cubs were gathered in the schoolyard, waiting for the morning bell to ring. Barry was right: a rumor had indeed been going around about an announcement. But it had been started by Too-Tall himself. That way, once everyone was buzzing about the upcoming announcement, Too-Tall could step in and make his own dramatic announcement about the announcement. Nobody was sure how he found out about these things. Did he sneak around the school offices, listening in on conversations? Not likely. Did he have a ring of spies in the school administration? Even less likely. But somehow he always knew what was going to happen before it happened.

"So, tell us, Big Guy," said Queenie McBear, poking her on-again, off-again boyfriend in the stomach, "what's it about?"

"Swimming pool," said Too-Tall matter-of-factly.

"A swimming pool?" said Queenie. "You mean here at school?"

Too-Tall nodded.

"They're gonna build a swimming pool?" said Barry.

Too-Tall nodded again. "And you know what that means," he said.

"Swimming classes!" said Brother Bear.

"Maybe even a swimming *team!*" added Sister Bear.

"Oh, my...," said Ferdy Factual, putting a hand to his mouth. He looked worried.

That made Too-Tall chuckle. He had guessed that the new pool would cause great excitement among the student body— and great anxiety among the students *about* their bodies. Especially students like Nerdy

Ferdy. There was a school joke that Ferdy was a thirty-eight-pound weakling, and twenty pounds of *that* was his brain.

Skuzz couldn't wait to add to Ferdy's anxiety. "And the classes are gonna be code!" he said.

"Of course they'll be cold," said Barry. "Unless they give us a heated pool, that is."

"Don't pay no attention to Skuzz," said Too-Tall. "He's an idiot." He popped his deputy on the shoulder with a big fist. "You don't say it *code*, moron! It's *coed*. Co-ed. It means boys and girls together. Get it?"

"I *know* what it means," said Skuzz. "I just don't know how to *say* it."

"If I had a nickel for every thing you don't know," said Too-Tall, "I'd be richer than Squire Grizzly."

"Gee, I'd better get a bathing suit," said Ferdy to no one in particular.

"Now, don't panic, little guy," said Too-Tall. "Everybody's gotta wear school-issue black bathing suits."

"Oh, no!" gasped Queenie. "I wouldn't be caught dead in a school-issue black bathing suit!"

"Whaddya mean?" said Too-Tall. "You'd look good in a black bathing suit."

Queenie blushed in spite of herself. "Gee, thanks," she said. "But school-issue? They probably look like the suits my mother wears."

Too-Tall shrugged. "I've seen your mother in a bathing suit," he said, "and she don't look half bad."

"That's enough, you big oaf!" snapped Queenie. "You can flirt with me all you like, but how dare you flirt with my *mother!*" She stuck her nose in the air and stalked off.

Too-Tall looked puzzled. "Hey, what gives, Queen? Your mother ain't even here!" He looked at his gang. "What was I supposed to say? That her mother's ugly?"

"No, boss," said Vinnie.

"Of course not," said Smirk.

"She's just a fickle girl," added Skuzz.

"Skuzz, dear," said Bonnie Brown, "a guy

who can't pronounce 'coed' shouldn't use big words like 'fickle.' "

"Hey," said Too-Tall, "if I'd thought this pool thing would start a spat like this, I wouldn't have brought it up in the first place."

Now Queenie came slinking back. "I'm sorry, Big Guy," she cooed. "I know you didn't mean it. So, who's gonna be the swimming teacher?"

"Now I ain't tellin' ya," said Too-Tall.

Queenie grabbed Too-Tall's left arm and twisted it.

"Not even if you twist my arm," said Too-Tall.

Queenie twisted a little harder, but then stopped because the bell had just rung to start the school day.

Chapter 2
"Why, When *I* Was in School..."

As usual, Too-Tall turned out to be right. Before classes started, there was a special announcement over the loudspeaker from Mr. Honeycomb, the principal. And it was indeed about the construction of an indoor swimming pool, to be completed in less than two weeks. The announcement closed with some details about swimming classes and tryouts for the new swimming team.

By the time Brother and Sister got home from school, they were almost talked out about the new pool. But they had enough left to tell Mama and Papa, and also Grizzly Gramps and Grizzly Gran, who had come over for dinner.

"Hey, guess what?" cried Sister as she and Brother burst into the family room, where the grownups were chatting.

"Haven't the faintest idea," said Gramps, with a wink at Gran.

"Me neither," said Gran, with a wink at Mama.

"I'll take a crack at it," said Papa, looking up from the afternoon newspaper. "Bear Country School is going to have a swimming pool."

"How did you know?" said Brother.

"Says so right here in the *Beartown Gazette*," said Papa. He read: " 'Bear Country School's new swimming pool will be finished soon. Coed swim classes will be taught by Mr. Mervyn Grizzmeyer, who will also coach the new swimming team.' "

Mervyn "Bullhorn" Grizzmeyer was the

school's vice principal and general sports coach. He was nicknamed Bullhorn because he didn't need one.

"Merv'll be a great swimming coach," said Gramps.

"Gee, I don't know about that," said Sister.

"Why not?" asked Mama. "What's wrong with Mr. Grizzmeyer?"

"I just can't get used to the idea of Mr. G in a bathing suit," said Sister. "He's not exactly the male model type."

"That's because he's *not* a male model," said Papa. "He's a vice principal and a coach. Heck, if that's your only complaint, I'd say things look pretty rosy."

"Well, there is one other thing…," said Sister.

"What's that?" said Papa.

Sister seemed embarrassed to tell them.

So Brother did it for her. "All the girls are upset because we have to wear school-issue black bathing suits," he said.

"Oh, my goodness! What a disaster!" said Papa in a sarcastic voice. "What do you think they're running over there—a country club? Why, when *I* was in school, we were lucky to have running water!"

"And when *I* was in school," said Gramps, "we were lucky to have indoor plumbing!"

"Sister, I should think you'd be more concerned about making the team than about your bathing suit," scolded Papa.

"Sis?" said Brother. "On the swimming team?"

"Why not?" said Papa. "Last summer, if I remember correctly, she turned herself into a pretty good little swimmer."

"*Pretty* good?" said Sister. "*Little?*"

"It's just an expression, dear," said Mama.

"Papa knows you're a big girl and an excellent swimmer."

"Oh, come off it," said Brother. "No offense, Sis, but you're younger and smaller than all the other cubs who'll be trying out for the team. Let's see now—I'll make the team for my crawl, Cousin Fred will make it for his backstroke, Queenie for her butterfly, and Bonnie for her breaststroke. Unless, that is, Too-Tall and the gang beat us all out."

"You mean," said Sister, "unless *I* beat you all out."

Brother looked at Sister in mock amazement. Then he threw his head back and laughed. It wasn't a real, spontaneous laugh. It was a fake laugh, designed to make Sister feel ridiculous.

"All right, Brother," said Mama, "that'll be enough of that. You cubs come help me and Gran get dinner ready. The men can set the dining room table later."

"*And* do the dishes," added Gran.

"I'll dry!" said Gramps before Papa could.

Chapter 3
Breaking In the Pool

Quicker than you can say "butterfly stroke," the new pool was finished. Teacher Bob's class had the honor of breaking it in. But there was a big downside to this honor: it meant they were scheduled for swimming class during the day's first period. Fall was moving on toward winter, and it wasn't exactly the most pleasant thing in the world to go straight from the nippy morning air to the even nippier morning pool water. Changing into their bathing suits so early in the morning was bad enough, but on the way from the locker rooms to the pool, the cubs had to walk through an ankle-deep chemical bath to clean their feet. And the chemical bath was even colder than the pool water. So by the time they got to the pool, they were all shivering. A few couldn't keep their teeth from chattering.

Mr. Grizzmeyer had the cubs sit on the benches that lined the walls on either side of the pool, boys on one side and girls on

the other. Some of the girls couldn't help giggling at the sight of their vice principal in a bathing suit.

"Care to share what's so funny with the rest of us?" said Mr. Grizzmeyer.

"We weren't giggling," said Queenie quickly. "We were—er, whimpering. Yeah, that's it—'cause it's so cold in here!"

"The only thing worse than giggling in swimming class is whimpering," Mr. Grizzmeyer said sternly. "I'll have no more of it. Now, line up at poolside, boys facing girls. We're going to start off with a simple dive and a lap back and forth across the pool. You can use any stroke you want. Boys first. Oh, I almost forgot: is there anyone here who can't swim?"

No one answered.

"Okay, boys," said Mr. Grizzmeyer. "On the count of three, dive in. One…two…*three!*"

The boys dived into the water and headed across the pool, some using the crawl, others using the backstroke or the sidestroke. All except for Vinnie, one of Too-Tall's gang members. He was still poised for his dive when most of the other cubs had half finished their laps.

"Let's go, Vinnie!" barked Mr. Grizzmeyer. "We haven't got all day!"

Vinnie made an awkward dive. But when

he came up, all he did was wave his arms
and slap at the water.

"What stroke is Vinnie using?" Brother
asked Fred as they climbed out of the pool
at the end of their lap.

"I think it's called the flail," cracked Fred.

"Hey!" said Brother. "He's not swimming,
he's *drowning!*"

Even as Brother spoke, Mr. Grizzmeyer was swimming toward Vinnie with strong, sure strokes. Within seconds, he hauled the shaken cub to safety. The entire class applauded the rescue, except for Too-Tall, Skuzz, and Smirk, who still hadn't finished their laps. It looked as if the Too-Tall gang weren't going to be the stars of the swimming team after all.

"Vinnie, you nitwit!" roared Mr. Grizzmeyer. "I just asked if anyone here can't swim! Why didn't you speak up?"

Vinnie sat at the edge of the pool, gasping for air. "I...I wasn't sure...if I could swim or not," he said between gasps.

"Why the heck not?" said Mr. Grizzmeyer.

"Because I never tried," said Vinnie.

Mr. Grizzmeyer rolled his eyes as the whole class burst into laughter. "Vinnie, you're dismissed from class," said Mr. Grizzmeyer. "I'll sign you up for after-school swimming instruction. When you catch your breath, get dressed and report back to Teacher Bob."

The rest of class went swimmingly, so to speak. Except for two glitches. Both came during the free time at the end of the period. The first was when Bertha Broom did a belly flop off the low diving board. (No one was allowed on the high dive yet, and certainly not for belly flops.) She hit the surface like a ton of bricks and knocked so much water out of the pool that Mr. Grizzmeyer had to add some before the next class.

The second glitch came while Barry Bruin was treading water in the deep end.

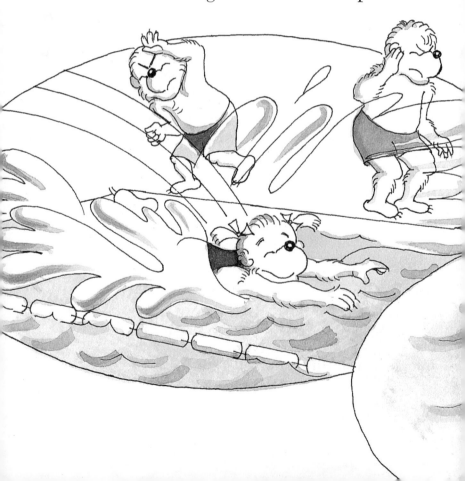

Too-Tall sneaked up underneath him and
yanked his bathing suit off. Before Barry
could snatch it back, Too-Tall rolled it into a
ball and threw it into the stands. The class
laughed hysterically.

Mr. Grizzmeyer ordered Too-Tall to climb into the stands to retrieve Barry's bathing suit, then kicked him out of class. "Go to my office and wait for me!" he said.

"Mr. G?" said Too-Tall. "Can I stop at my locker on the way to get my Game Bear?"

"What do you think my office is?" growled Mr. Grizzmeyer. "An entertainment center?"

Too-Tall shrugged. "Can't blame a guy for tryin'," he said. And off he strutted, with a wave to his snickering gang.

Chapter 4
Tryouts

The next day after school, cubs gathered at the pool for swimming team tryouts. This time the boys and girls weren't separated. Mr. Grizzmeyer wasn't present yet, so they sat wherever they liked on either bench. Bonnie Brown sat with her best friend, Brother Bear.

"Oh, look," said Bonnie, nodding at the bench on the opposite side of the pool. "It's your little sister and her friend Lizzy Bruin. Aren't they kind of young to be trying out for the team?"

"Tell me about it," said Brother. "It's all my dad's fault."

"How's that?" said Bonnie.

"He pushed her to try out," said Brother. "He pumped up her ego like crazy, and of course Mama agreed with him to spare Sis's feelings."

"Uh-oh," said Bonnie. "I'm afraid she's in for a disappointment."

"In a way, it's my fault, too," Brother admitted. "When she took Papa's bait about trying out, I teased her. I thought that might stop her, but it boomeranged."

"How do you mean?" asked Bonnie.

"Teasing her just made her more deter-
mined to try out," said Brother. "You know,
to prove me wrong. I'll bet she and Lizzy
finish so far behind everybody else that they
get laughed at. She's gonna wind up in
tears. Hey, where's our coach, anyway?"

As if on cue, Mr. Grizzmeyer emerged
from his private locker room and strode to
poolside. As he surveyed the collection of
would-be team members, his gaze came to
rest on one cub in particular.

"Too-Tall," he said, "what do you call
those things on your feet?"

Some of the cubs snickered.

"Things?" said Too-Tall. "What things?"
He looked down. "Oh, *those* things. They're
flippers."

Mr. Grizzmeyer shook his head. "No

flippers in tryouts," he said.

Too-Tall pretended to look shocked. "No flippers?" he said. "Why not, Coach?"

"They'll give you an unfair advantage over the other cubs," said Mr. Grizzmeyer.

"I don't see why it's unfair," said Too-Tall.

"If the rest of these clowns had any brains, they would have worn flippers, too."

"Get rid of 'em," said Mr. Grizzmeyer. "End of discussion."

Too-Tall took off his flippers and slid them under the bench.

"All right, cubs," said the coach. "Tryouts for the swimming team will now begin." He held up a stopwatch. "I'm going to time you in each event you try out for. You'll go three at a time, and I'll get an exact time for the winner in each heat. I can estimate the other swimmers' times from how far they finish behind the winner. First, freestyle."

Brother, Too-Tall, and Skuzz were in the first heat. Though Too-Tall was good at most sports, swimming was clearly not his thing, as he'd shown already in swimming class. Without his flippers, he kept sinking. And Skuzz was even worse. His performance reminded everyone that another name for freestyle is "the crawl." He was so slow that he indeed looked as if he were crawling through the water. Brother won with ease.

"Excellent time, Brother," said Coach Grizzmeyer. "That'll be hard to beat."

And hard to beat it was. By the end of

the next-to-last freestyle heat, no one had even come close. And the last heat obviously wouldn't present much of a challenge to Brother's time, because only Sister Bear, Lizzy Bruin, and Babs Bruno were left. Sister and Lizzy were both two years younger than Brother, and Babs had never been much of an athlete. In fact, Babs had told

Queenie that she was only at tryouts so she could watch the boys race.

Brother felt a little jittery as his sister took her place at the edge of the pool. He crossed his fingers. He knew Sister wouldn't get a good time, but at least she might beat Lizzy and Babs.

Mr. Grizzmeyer counted to three, and off they went. Babs's dive was more of a fall than a dive, and she went down like a stone.

She had to push off the bottom of the pool, and by the time she surfaced, she was already way behind Lizzy. Lizzy, in turn, was already way behind Sister. Not because Lizzy was such a bad swimmer, but because Sister was so good.

"Hey, look at her go!" said Bonnie.

"Yeah!" said Brother. "She's faster than I thought. A *lot* faster!"

Sister cut through the water like a cross between a shark and a torpedo. Mr. Grizzmeyer couldn't even wait for the end of the heat to congratulate her. The moment she emerged from the pool, with Lizzy and Babs still struggling to finish, he

cried, "Wow! You just beat your brother by four full seconds! Sister, you're the team's number one freestyler!"

As Queenie and Bertha cheered and whistled, Too-Tall and Skuzz razzed Brother with a string of horselaughs. But Bonnie wasn't sure how to act. On her best friend's face was an expression that reflected both the thrill of Sister's victory and the agony of his own defeat. "At least she didn't end up crying" was all Bonnie could think of to say.

"I'm glad she didn't end up crying," said Brother. "On the other hand, I'm not exactly thrilled that I just got creamed in my best event by my own little sister."

But Sister wasn't done yet, not by a long shot. The other top swimmers in Teacher Bob's class—Bonnie, Fred, and Queenie— all got beaten by Sister in their main events. That meant that Sister was not only the team's top freestyler but also its top breast-stroker, backstroker, and butterflyer.

"Sister Bear, you're a regular phenom!" gushed Mr. Grizzmeyer. "I've never seen anything like it! How about I call your dad right away? He'll be thrilled!"

Sister beamed up at Mr. Grizzmeyer. "Sure, Coach," she said. "Go ahead."

"Oh, no," groaned Brother.

"What's wrong?" asked Bonnie as they stood up and got ready to head for opposite locker rooms.

"I know *I* can handle this," said Brother. "But what about Papa?"

Chapter 5
A Hero's Welcome

Brother's hunch proved all too true, of course. Papa had planned to pick the cubs up in the family car after the tryouts, but Mama showed up instead. When the cubs asked her why Papa hadn't come, she just said, "Oh, you'll see when we get home."

As the red roadster pulled into the tree-house driveway in the twilight, the cubs noticed that the house was much brighter than usual. That was because it was lit up not only inside but outside, too. In the brief time it had taken Mama to pick the cubs up at school, Papa had dug the Christmas

tree lights out of a closet, hauled the stepladder up from the basement, and climbed around like an acrobat to hang the multicolored lights all over the house. What's more, he had hand-painted a big poster-paper banner and nailed it above the front door. In big black letters lit up by a dangling floodlight, the banner read: CONGRATULATIONS, FAMILY PHENOM!!!

The moment Mama turned off the car, Papa burst from the front door, threw his hands in the air, and yelled, "Hooray for Sister! Hip, hip, hooray!" He bounded down the steps and caught Sister up in his arms as she got out of the car. "My little girl!" he cried. "I mean, my *big* girl! I knew you could do it! You're great! You're terrific! You're going to win every heat in every meet! And I'm going to be there to cheer you on!"

As he put Sister down, Papa noticed Brother climbing out of the car. He reached over and gave his son a little pat on the back. "Nice going, son," he said. "Coach said you had the second-best time in the crawl. That means we've got the top two freestylers right here in the family. What's wrong, son? You don't look very excited."

Brother just shrugged.

"I think Brother may be a bit over-whelmed by all this," Mama whispered into Papa's ear.

But Brother overheard. "I'm not over-whelmed," he said.

"No kidding," said Papa. "From looking at you, I'd say you're *under*whelmed."

"No again," said Brother. "I'm not over-whelmed, and I'm not underwhelmed. I'm just...whelmed."

And with that, Brother shuffled up the steps and into the house.

"Now, what do you suppose is eatin' him?" said Papa, looking at Mama.

"Dear," she said, "I think we'd better have a talk about that right now."

"Okay," said Papa. "But it'll have to wait until after dinner—even later, in fact. Because after dinner, I'm taking Sister to the Beartown Community Center pool for a special practice session. The pool closes at eight, so we have to hurry."

"Special practice session?" said Sister.

"Yep," said Papa. "I'm going to be your personal trainer."

"But I already *have* a swimming coach—"

"And an excellent one, too," said Papa. "But a coach isn't a personal trainer. And you, my dear, have so much potential that you need extra attention. *And* extra work!"

"But, Papa," said Sister, "I'm really tired from tryouts..."

"Oh, come now!" said Papa. "That's no way for a champion swimmer to talk!" He gazed dreamily up into the darkening sky and spied the first evening star. "Look!" he said. "Make a wish..."

Papa, Mama, and Sister closed their eyes and concentrated. Usually, when the family made wishes, Papa wanted to know right away what everyone had wished for. But not this time. "I'll tell you what I wished for," he said. "I wished for a gold medal in the

Bearlympics for my little girl. Er, I mean, my *big* girl. And believe you me, Sister, when you're standing proudly on that highest pedestal, listening to the Bear Country national anthem, with that gold medal hanging around your neck, you'll thank me a thousand times over for all the extra work I made you do! Now let's hurry up and eat while there's time to get that workout in."

As Papa bounded up the steps into the house, Mama turned to look into her daughter's confused face. Sister gazed up into Mama's eyes. Mama didn't even have to say anything. Her eyes said it all, and what they said went something like this: "You know your papa, dear—how excited he gets about your victories and achievements. But don't worry; he'll calm down in a day or two."

Sister smiled at Mama, and arm in arm, they climbed the tree-house steps.

Chapter 6
Overboard

Papa didn't get around to having a talk with Mama that evening. He was so worn out from hanging the Christmas lights and the banner and from spending part of the evening as Sister's personal trainer that he went straight to bed when he got home from the public pool. Nor did he have time to talk with Mama the next morning after the cubs got off to school, because he was swamped with orders for furniture.

In fact, it wasn't until late afternoon, when Papa came in from his workshop to wash up and change before heading for swimming practice, that Mama finally demanded some attention.

"Oh, all right," said Papa. "But make it quick, 'cause I'm in a hurry. Now, what's it about?"

"What's it about?" gasped Mama. "Have you forgotten already, dear? It's about Brother moping around ever since the swimming tryouts last night."

"Oh, that," said Papa. "Did you ask him what's bothering him?"

"I didn't *have* to ask him," said Mama. "It's as plain as the nose on his face. He feels left out."

"Left out?" said Papa. "You mean because of Sister's success? But I congratulated him for his crawl time."

Mama rolled her eyes and sighed. "Dear," she said, "a little pat on the back can hardly compare with colored lights, banners, and 'Hooray for Sister!' "

"And why should it?" said Papa. "Brother didn't get the top times in all four main events. He doesn't *deserve* all the fuss Sister does. He's two years older than Sister, so he ought to understand."

"Dear, he may be two years older than Sister," said Mama, "but he's still a cub. A cub doesn't think, 'Gee, my sister did ten times better than I did, so she deserves ten times the praise I do.' In fact, *nobody* thinks like that."

Suddenly, Papa looked sheepish. "You're right, dear," he said. "I guess I kind of went overboard."

"*Kind of?*" said Mama. "Are you joking?"

"Okay, okay," Papa mumbled. "I already went overboard; you don't have to make me walk the plank, too."

Mama smiled and said, "I'm sorry, dear. I guess I should be thankful you've seen the error of your ways so soon."

Papa's expression changed from sheepish to sincere. "And I have," he said. "I'll try to balance things out a little better between Brother and Sister. You know, root for both of them."

But then that slightly crazed twinkle danced into Papa's eyes again. "But Sister's success doesn't have to mean Brother's failure, you know," he continued. "Why, if she gets a swimming scholarship to the college of her choice, we can afford to send Brother wherever *he* wants to go, too!"

"Now, wait a minute, dear," said Mama.

"Don't count your scholarships before they're hatched. Sister's still so young. There's no telling how she'll feel about swimming when it comes time to go to college."

"And that's *exactly* why we have to push her now!" cried Papa. "So she'll achieve greatness! So she can go to her favorite college *and* win the Bearlympics!"

"But that's all so far in the future," said Mama. "Right now, what's important about swimming for Sister is that she enjoy it."

"And she will!" insisted Papa. "What little cub wouldn't enjoy winning a gold medal at the Bearlympics?"

"That's just my point, dear," said Mama. "*Little* cubs don't compete in the Bearlympics. Big cubs and grownups do."

"If that's your point, I don't get it," said Papa. He glanced at his watch. "Wow! I'm gonna be late for practice!" And he dashed down the front steps to the red roadster.

As Mama watched the family car raise a trail of dust on the sunny dirt road to downtown Beartown, she shook her head and sighed. Hadn't she wanted Papa to see the error of his ways? And hadn't he done exactly that, and apologized, too? Then why was she left with the funny feeling that she hadn't gotten through to him at all?

Chapter 7
A Word of Caution

The very first swimming practice played to an audience of just one. But what a one! Papa Bear made enough noise for a hundred bears. He ranted, he raved. He jumped up and down in the stands, yelling "Go, Sister!" every time she got up off the

bench. Once, when it turned out she had only gotten up to go to the bathroom, Papa's yell brought a chorus of laughter from the team. Even Coach Grizzmeyer had to stifle a chuckle. But Sister wasn't laughing. When she came back from the bathroom, she shot Papa a nasty look and then refused to look at him again for the rest of practice.

Papa didn't take the hint, however. He thought Sister was just redoubling her concentration for the last freestyle heat. He did remember to cheer "Go, Sister! Go, Brother!" during the heat, but it was pretty obvious to everyone that Sister was his favorite.

Sister won every heat in every event, but in the last butterfly heat, she beat Queenie by barely a nose. And the final freestyle heat was another photo finish, with Brother almost tying Sister.

Coach Grizzmeyer looked concerned as he came over to Sister after that last heat. "What's wrong, kid?" he said. "Your times have all fallen off. Way off. You look tired, like you can't get your wind."

Sister was indeed breathing much harder

than she had after the tryout heats. Between breaths, she told the coach about her extra practice session the night before.

"Well, that's got to stop" was Coach Grizzmeyer's firm reply.

"But I didn't want to do it," said Sister. "Papa made me."

"Don't worry," said the coach. "I'll take care of Papa. Go get changed."

When Sister had disappeared into the locker room, Coach Grizzmeyer motioned Papa to the edge of the stands. Papa thought the coach wanted to thank him for taking the time to be Sister's personal trainer, so he leaned over the railing and said, "I know what you're gonna say, Coach. But no thanks are necessary. I'll do anything to help my little girl win a gold or three or four at the Bearlympics. I'll be the engine of her success!"

"Well, if you're going to be the engine," said Mr. Grizzmeyer, "then I'll have to be the brake. You're pushing her too hard, Papa. The cub's exhausted from that extra practice session last night."

"I just thought she'd benefit from a little extra work," said Papa.

"Tell you what," said the coach. "Let me worry about the work, and you can worry about her being healthy and happy. Don't forget, she's a lot younger than anyone else on the team."

"Whatever you say, Coach," said Papa. "She's in your hands. I'll just come to all the practices to cheer her on."

"In that case," said Mr. Grizzmeyer, "I'll be more than the brake; I'll be the muffler, too. If you come to practices, you're going to have to keep it down a little. All that yelling and screaming for Sister isn't really fair to the other team members."

"Sure thing, Coach," said Papa as Mr. Grizzmeyer turned and headed for his locker room. "See you tomorrow!"

With his back turned to Papa, Coach Grizzmeyer rolled his eyes and muttered, "I can hardly wait."

Chapter 8
The Big Meet

Papa did tone down his act at practices, but at home he continued to talk endlessly about Sister's bright future as a champion swimmer. Sister was moodier than usual, but her heat times did improve. And Papa was very glad of that, because the team's first meet of the season was almost upon them. During the week leading up to the meet, he pushed Sister constantly, telling her over and over how important it was to get her career off to a good start.

Almost before they knew it, it was time for the big meet. The Bearville team was visiting Bear Country School. Bearville was known to have a strong swimming team, with one cub in particular who might be Sister's equal in the breaststroke and the butterfly. Papa thought that was the reason Sister seemed a little glum on the evening of the meet.

"Cheer up, dear," he told her as they drove to school for the meet. "No Bearville swimmer can beat you. I guarantee it." He lowered his voice so as not to be overheard by Brother, who was stretched out on the back seat, trying to relax before the meet. "And we already know for sure that no Bear

Country School swimmer can beat you."

"I know, I know," said Sister in a distracted tone of voice.

"Good," said Papa. "But from the sound of your voice, I'd say your mind is off somewhere else."

"I was thinking about how it would be fun to play jacks with Lizzy after school tomorrow," said Sister.

"For heaven's sake, Sister!" said Papa. "You've got to put childish things like that out of your mind! You're about to compete in your first swim meet. Focus on that. Remember what I told you: you've got to do your best tonight because—"

"I know, I know," said Sister, cutting Papa off. "Because tonight this meet is the most important thing in my life. Don't worry. I can't play jacks after school tomorrow anyway, 'cause I have swimming practice."

Earlier that day, Papa had hand-lettered a placard to take to the meet. It said:

IT'S RUDE, IT'S CRUDE, IT JUST AIN'T FAIR TO HAVE TO SWIM AGAINST SISTER BEAR!

But when Mama had seen it, she'd put her foot down. She snatched a black marker from a kitchen drawer, blacked out Papa's jingle, and printed something on the other side of the placard. Then she held it up for Papa's inspection.

" 'SISTER AND BROTHER BEAR! WHAT A PAIR!' " read Papa. "But, dear! That's so lame!"

"Lame or not, that's what it's going to be," said Mama. "Unless you can come up with something better."

"But I already came up with something better!" said Papa.

"I mean something better *that meets my approval*," said Mama.

Knowing it was hopeless to argue, Papa gave in. But the "lameness" of the placard certainly didn't keep him from waving it around at the swim meet. The parents sitting behind were pretty annoyed. But no one was more annoyed than Mama. That was because every time Papa waved the placard back and forth, it hit Mama in the head.

Though Papa's antics in the stands attracted a lot of attention, Sister's performance in the pool attracted more. She won all four of her events and almost single-handedly won the meet for Bear Country School. In the end, the rest of the team lifted her onto their shoulders and carried her around the pool to wild applause from the audience. Mama had to grab Papa's arm to keep him from jumping out of the stands to join in the poolside celebration.

Chapter 9
Victory Pizza

After the swim meet, Papa and Mama took the whole team, including Coach Grizzmeyer and a bunch of the other parents, out for pizza. As their cars pulled into the Pizza Shack parking lot, Mama did a double take. "Where did *that* come from?" she said, pointing to a banner hanging above the entrance. In huge letters, it read: CONGRATULATIONS, B.C.S. SWIMMERS!

Below that, it said: AND HOORAY FOR THE
BEAR FAMILY PHENOM!

"Oh, that," said Papa. "I brought it over

this afternoon. I had a feeling we were going to win tonight."

Inside, they shared a dozen large deluxe specials with everything but anchovies. Except for Coach Grizzmeyer, who was a confirmed anchovy lover. He had his own

pizza, just with extra anchovies. Everyone had a great time, even Brother, who had finished second only to Sister in the crawl, beating all the Bearville swimmers. That seemed to have given him a dose of team spirit at last.

Brother was whooping it up with the other cubs when, all of a sudden, he noticed that Sister didn't seem to be having as good a time as everyone else. She was smiling, but not laughing and joking. And it looked

as if she were faking the smile. So he leaned over and said, "What's wrong, Sis? I thought you'd be dancing on the table by now."

"Oh, it's nothing," she said. "I'm fine."

"Wait, I bet I know what it is," said Brother. "You left your homework until after the meet, and now you're afraid you'll be too tired to do it. Don't worry, I'll help you."

"No thanks," said Sister. "I'll just get up early tomorrow and do it before school."

"Oh, sure," said Brother. "Okay." But he knew she was lying. Sister was a sound sleeper who had never gotten up early a day in her life. And she'd be extra worn out after the meet.

Gee, thought Brother, *I wonder what's going on with her.*

It was the first and only sign of the disaster to come.

Chapter 10
Good News and Bad News

The great hammer blow of fate fell the very next morning, right after Brother and Sister had left for school. The phone rang, and Papa answered it.

"Good morning, Coach," he said. "I wasn't expecting to hear your voice again until this afternoon's practice...What? What do you mean, no practice for me?... Yes...Yes...Oh, my goodness. I see, yes... good-bye..."

"Don't tell me you've gotten yourself banned from practice," said Mama, hands on hips.

Papa just stood by the phone, the

receiver still in his hand. He had a look of utter horror on his face. "No," he managed. "It's worse than that."

"Worse?" said Mama, taking the receiver from Papa and replacing it. "What did Coach Grizzmeyer say?"

"He said he had good news and bad news," murmured Papa.

"What's the good news?" asked Mama.

"Sister's crawl time last night set a new league record."

"My goodness!" said Mama. "That's wonderful! But what's the bad news?"

Papa swallowed hard. "She's off the team."

"Off the team?" gasped Mama. "Why?"

"Teacher Jane just sent in the grades for the term," said Papa. "Sister's are so bad that she's not allowed to swim with the team until she pulls them up. We have to go meet with Teacher Jane during morning recess."

"Oh, dear," said Mama. She looked down at her nightgown. "I'd better get dressed." As she headed upstairs to the bedroom, she muttered, "I was afraid of something like this…"

Chapter 11
Parent-Teacher Conference

What Teacher Jane showed Mama and Papa at their conference shocked them. On her desk, Teacher Jane spread out all of Sister's math tests for the term. Sister had gotten A's and B's until the final exam, which counted triple. On the final, she'd missed more than half the questions, giving her an F. That meant she had dropped to a D+ for the term.

"I don't understand it," said Papa, staring at Sister's final exam. "That's not like our daughter at all. She knows her multiplication tables backward and forward!"

"Now have a look at these," said Teacher

Jane, spreading Sister's spelling tests across the desk.

"Hmm," said Mama. "B, B, A, A...F. My goodness! That averages out to just a C-, because the final counts triple."

Teacher Jane nodded. She pointed to an answer on the final and an answer on one of the earlier tests. "See these?" she said. "On the final, Sister added an *e* to 'potato.' But

earlier, she got it right. What might cause her to do something like that?"

"Maybe she just forgot?" said Papa.

Teacher Jane shook her head. "I really shouldn't beat around the bush," she said. "I've talked with Coach Grizzmeyer and—"

"It's the swimming team," Mama interrupted. "I was afraid something like this might happen."

"All right, all right," said Papa quickly. "I admit it. It's my fault. I've been putting too much pressure on her."

Teacher Jane nodded. "I must say, it takes a big bear to admit a thing like that."

"Wrong," said Papa. "It only takes a bear who has his daughter's best interests at heart. And that's why I'm going to drill her until she pulls her grades up and gets back on the team. To lessen the pressure, I'll have her compete in just two events instead of four from now on. Why, she can still get a swimming scholarship on two events. And it'll just mean two gold medals instead of four at the Bearlympics. I can live with that."

"But the question is, can Sister live with it?" said Mama.

"What do you mean, dear?" asked Papa.

"I mean two events instead of four is still

two more than any cub Sister's age has ever competed in," said Mama.

Papa snapped his fingers. "Piece o' cake," he said. "And with me drilling her in all her school subjects, her grades will be back up in no time. She'll only miss one meet—two at the most."

PIECE O' CAKE.

Teacher Jane looked a little leery of Papa's proposal, but he seemed so keen on it that she didn't want to challenge him. "I'm not so sure this will work," she said, "but I guess it's worth a try."

"All right," said Mama. "Let's try it. But, dear, you have to remember to be patient with Sister."

"Patient?" said Papa. "I ask you: who's more patient than Papa Q. Bear? Now, hurry up, dear. We've got to get home so I can make Sister's flash cards!"

And with that, Papa dashed out of the classroom without so much as a good-bye to Teacher Jane.

Mama rose and gave Teacher Jane a look that said, "There he goes again. Don't worry, I'll handle it." And she walked calmly after her husband.

Chapter 12
"P-o-t-a-t"

When Sister got home from school that afternoon, Mama noticed that she seemed happier and more relaxed than she'd been in weeks. But as soon as Papa told her about his plan to get her back on the team, her face fell. "Oh, great," she said. "I'm gonna go play jacks with Lizzy. Bye."

"Now, wait a minute, honey," said Papa. "We need to get started on your math and spelling drills right away. Go on up to your room, and I'll be up with the flash cards in a minute."

Sister heaved a sigh and trudged up the stairs. Papa grabbed his pile of flash cards.

"What did I say about patience, dear?" said Mama.

"Oh, right," said Papa. He called up the stairs, "Relax for a while, champ! No rush! I'm going to read the paper first!"

Papa picked up the *Beartown Gazette*

and pretended to read it for a few seconds. Then he threw it down and bounded up the stairs two at a time, clutching his precious flash cards.

Mama shook her head and went into the kitchen to put the kettle on for tea. Ten minutes later, as she was sitting at the kitchen table sipping her tea, Papa came stomping in. Mama looked up into his flustered face and said, "Well?"

"It makes no sense!" Papa sputtered. "First she says five times seven is thirty-seven, and the next time she says it's thirty-three! She even missed three times four! She's hopeless!"

"Calm down, dear," said Mama. "You won't make any progress with her by getting all upset."

Papa took a deep breath. "You're right," he said. "I'll switch to spelling. We'll do math later." And back upstairs he went.

Five minutes later, Papa was back in the kitchen, more flustered than the first time. "It's no use!" he moaned. "She added an *e* to 'potato,' so I showed her the correct spelling. When I came back to it, she left off the *e*. But she dropped the *o*, too! She's probably the only cub who's ever spelled 'potato' *p-o-t-a-t!*"

Mama rose. "Sit down, dear," she said. "I think I know what the problem is. I'll go up and have a heart-to-heart with her."

Papa's furrowed brow smoothed a little. He let out a huge sigh of relief. "You will?" he said. "Thank heavens!" He sprawled, exhausted, in a kitchen chair while Mama went upstairs.

Sister was sitting on her bed with her legs folded under her. She looked up warily when Mama came into the room.

"You gonna drill me, too?" she asked.

"No," said Mama. "I just want to talk with you."

Sister sighed. "Okay," she said.

Mama had always been better than Papa at finding out what was bothering the cubs. In no time, Sister had admitted that she'd done poorly on her finals on purpose. Then she poured her heart out.

"I hate the swimming team!" she said, tears welling up in her eyes. "Swim, swim, swim! Just because you can do something well doesn't mean you should have to do it all the time! Besides, I'm getting waterlogged! I'm all wrinkled up like a prune! And I can't get the smell of chlorine out of my fur! I want to go back to playing jacks and jumping rope and picking wildflowers—stuff like that! Can't you understand that, Mama?"

Mama smiled. "Yes, I can," she said. "And after I explain it to Papa, he will, too. I promise."

Sister's face broke into a big grin. But

suddenly, the grin faded. "But what about Brother?" she said. "Won't he be disappointed in me?"

"Brother will be as happy as a clam," said Mama. "He'll be the number one freestyler on the team now."

"Oh, yeah!" said Sister. And she bounced off the bed and gave Mama a great big hug.

Chapter 13
Making the Grade

Papa's jaw dropped when Mama told him that Sister had cheated on her final exams—not to succeed but to fail. "It's unbelievable!" he said. "Sister has always been so proud of her good grades!"

"Yes, she has," said Mama. "And I'm sure it was very hard for her to fail on purpose. But it's not unbelievable. It just shows how badly she wanted off the swimming team."

"Wanted off the swimming team?" said Papa. "She never said anything about that to me."

"Of course she didn't," said Mama. "She

was afraid you'd blow your top. Or that you'd be crushed. After all, you already had her getting a swimming scholarship to college and winning gold medals at the Bearlympics. Can you imagine how much pressure she must have felt—not just to stay on the team, but to win every heat she swam? Under those conditions, being on the team couldn't have been much fun."

Papa looked horror-stricken. "Oh, my gosh!" he said, clapping a hand to his forehead. "What a dummy I've been! I just thought she'd naturally want to be a champion swimmer because she's so good at it."

"It's like anything else, dear," said Mama. "No matter how good at it you are, if it stops being fun, you won't want to do it anymore."

Papa put his head in his hands.

"She must be really mad at me," he

mumbled. "Maybe I should apologize..."

"Oh, I don't think it's as complicated as all that," said Mama. "If you don't hold it against Sister that she failed her finals on purpose, I'll bet she won't hold it against you that you pushed her so hard. Just wait and see. Here she comes…"

Sister's footsteps could be heard on the stairs. She came into the kitchen and looked hopefully up at her parents.

"Honey," said Mama with a smile, "your papa and I have decided that there's no rea-

son for you to be on the swimming team if you don't want to."

Sister's face lit up like a Christmas tree. "Yippee!" she cried.

"And," added Papa, "there's no need for any more drills. I'm sure you'll bring your grades back up all by yourself."

Sister ran to Papa and jumped into his arms. She gave him a big bear hug, then dropped to the floor and dashed to the front door. "I'm gonna go play jacks with Lizzy!" she said. "See ya later!"

From the kitchen window, Mama and Papa watched their daughter race down the sunny dirt road toward Lizzy's house.

"It's good to see her happy again," said Mama.

"It sure is," Papa agreed. "As for the swimming team, there's always next year." Out of the corner of his eye, he could see Mama looking suspiciously at him. "Or the *next* year...," he added.

"If?" Mama prompted him.

"Oh, right," said Papa. "*If* she wants to."

Mama smiled. "At least you're learning, dear," she said. She leaned over and kissed him on the cheek.

Papa grinned. "Well, you know what they say," he said. "Better late than never."

"Yes, it seems I've heard *that* somewhere before," said Mama. "I'm going to have another cup of tea. Would you like one?"

"Sure would," said Papa.

And together Mama and Papa went to put the kettle on. Even though it really was only a one-bear job.

Stan and Jan Berenstain began writing and illustrating books for children in the early 1960s, when their two young sons were beginning to read. That marked the start of the best-selling Berenstain Bears series. Now, with more than one hundred books in print, videos, television shows, and even Berenstain Bears attractions at major amusement parks, it's hard to tell where the Bears end and the Berenstains begin!

Stan and Jan make their home in Bucks County, Pennsylvania, near their sons—Leo, a writer, and Michael, an illustrator—who are helping them with Big Chapter Books stories and pictures. They plan on writing and illustrating many more books for children, especially for their four grandchildren, who keep them well in touch with the kids of today.